For Helen, with love
~P.B.

For Tom and Emily
~M.B.

Nobody Laughs at a Lion!

Paul Bright   *illustrated by* Matt Buckingham

Good Books

Intercourse, PA 17534
800/762-7171
www.goodbks.com

In the cool of the morning,
on the edge of the jungle, the
animals were busy as could be.
They were running and racing,
climbing and clambering, crawling
and creeping all over the place.
    Big Lion sat and watched.

"You can see why I'm King of the Jungle,"
he said. "It's because I'm the best."
"Do stop boasting," said Sister Lion. "And if
you are the best, what are you best at?"
Big Lion thought for a while.

"Well, running for a start. You just watch."
Big Lion bounded off through the long grass,
sending the other animals scattering in fright.

As Big Lion ran, the sleek, long-legged
Cheetah raced past him with ease.
Cheetah laughed. He laughed quietly,
because nobody laughs out loud at a lion.
But Big Lion heard him.

"All right," said Big Lion, rather annoyed. "Cheetah might be just a little bit better at running. But I'm best at . . . at climbing trees. Look!"

Big Lion dug his great claws into the nearest tree and scrambled and scratched and scrabbled, and slowly heaved himself up onto the lowest branch.

"Of course, some trees are more difficult to climb than others," he said.

Monkey was swinging by his tail in the highest branches of the tree. He saw Big Lion climbing and he sniggered. He sniggered quietly, because nobody sniggers out loud at a lion. But Big Lion heard him.

"All right," said Big Lion, grumpily.
"Monkey might be just a little bit better
at climbing trees. But I'm the best at . . .
at creeping through the long grass, quiet as quiet."

Big Lion dropped into a low crouch, then, crawling and creeping, slow as slow and quiet as quiet, he moved through the long grass.

Snake was slipping through the grass, smooth and silent as a sigh. He saw Big Lion crawling and creeping, and he smiled.

He smiled to himself, because nobody
smiles at a lion. But Big Lion saw him.

Big Lion was beginning to feel angry. "All right," he said.
"Snake might be just a little bit better at creeping
through the long grass, quiet as quiet. But I am
the best at . . . at . . ."

"You are very good at sleeping," said Sister Lion.

"Sleeping doesn't count," said Big Lion.

Then he said, "I am the strongest. Watch me." He pushed his great head against the trunk of a small tree, bending it until it broke with a loud crack!

Elephant was plodding past, leaving
a trail of flattened bushes and broken
trees in his path.

He saw Big Lion and he lifted his trunk
and trumpeted. He trumpeted softly,
because not even an elephant trumpets
out loud at a lion. But Big Lion heard him.

Now Big Lion was furious. "All right," he said. "Maybe Elephant is just a little bit stronger. But I am the best at . . . the best at . . . Oh! I can't think of anything!

"It really makes me want to . . .

". . . ROAR!"

And the sound of Big Lion's roar
rolled and rumbled and grew
and grumbled and echoed and
thundered through the jungle.

Big Lion really *was* the very, very
best at roaring.

Cheetah stopped laughing, and Monkey
stopped sniggering, and Snake stopped
smiling, and Elephant stopped trumpeting.

And Big Lion was happy at last . . . because
NOBODY laughs when the King of the Jungle roars!